A Boy and a House

A Boy and a House

Maja Kastelic

annick press
toronto + berkeley

Cataloging in Publication

Kastelic, Maja
[Deˇcek in hiˇsa. English]
A boy and a house / Maja Kastelic.

ISBN 978-1-77321-055-1 (hardcover).--ISBN 978-1-77321-054-4
(softcover)

1. Stories without words. I. Title. II.Title: Deˇcek in hiˇsa.
English

PZ7.1.K37Boy 2018   j891.8'436   C2018-901606-X

Published in the U.S.A. by Annick Press (U.S.) Ltd.
Distributed in Canada by University of Toronto Press.
Distributed in the U.S.A. by Publishers Group West.
Printed in China
www.annickpress.com
www.majakastelic.blogspot.com